by HARRIET ZIEFERT · Drawings by ELLIOT KRELOFF

MIGHTY

MAX!

BLUE APPLE BOOKS

For supermen and superboys–
Jon, James, Will, Nate and Charlie
-H.Z.

For Maggie
-E.K.

Distributed in the U.S. by Chronicle Books
First Edition
Printed in China

ISBN: 978-1-934706-36-7

1 3 5 7 9 10 8 6 4 2

Max heard his daddy shouting.

You're not **SUPERMAN.**
So climb down and sit.
You cannot be a bird
without hurting yourself.

Max sat.

But not for long.

Max sat.

"You're not **Evel Knievel!** So put your feet on the pedals before you lose control and crash into a tree."

Max's daddy said,
"If you're so mighty,
pick up the picnic basket
and put it in the back of the car.
We're going to the beach."

When they got there,
Max waited with
the beach stuff
while Daddy drove off
to park the car.

Max climbed
down the dune and
put the picnic basket
on the sand.

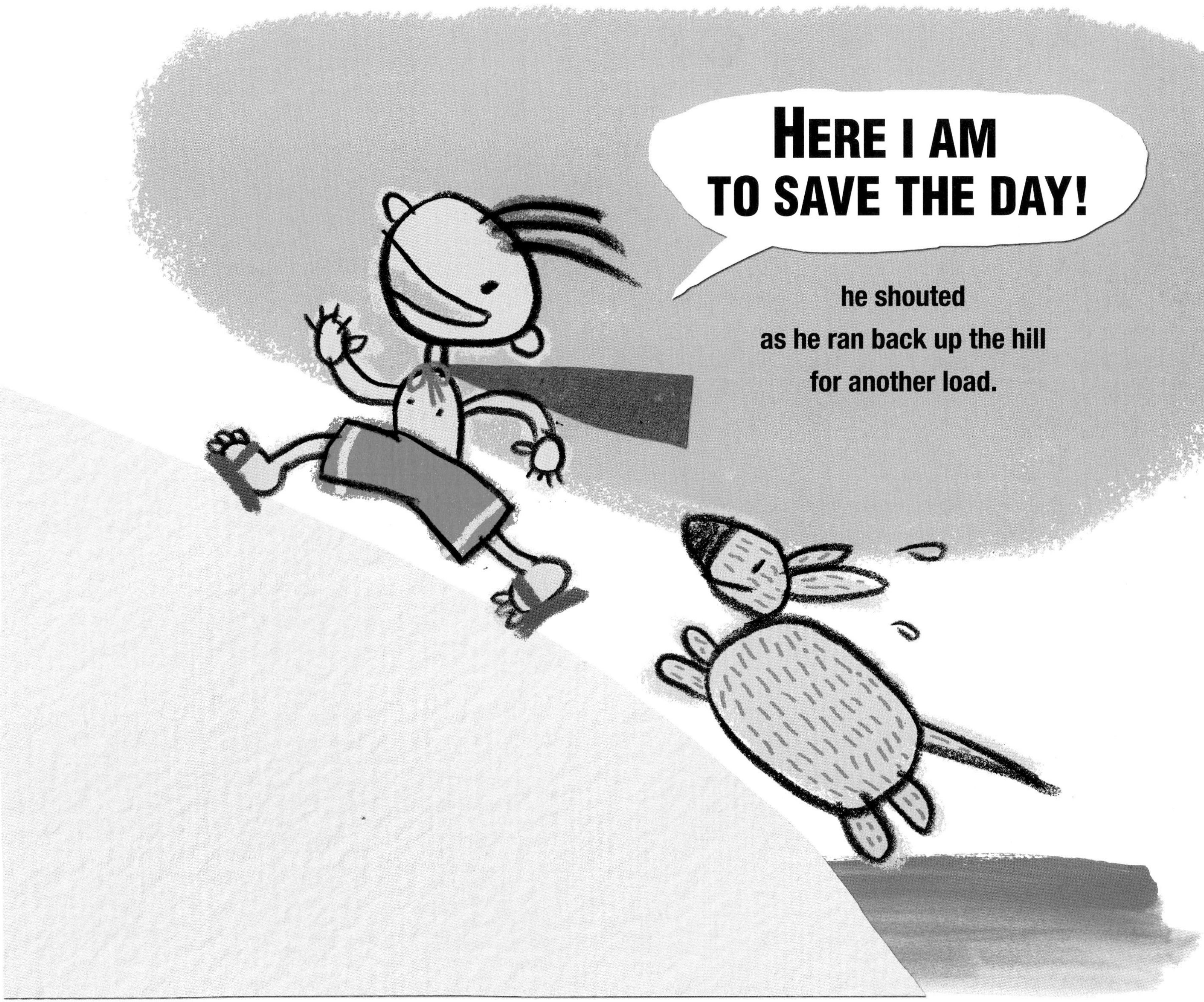

he shouted
as he ran back up the hill
for another load.

As soon as Daddy found a spot, Max climbed onto his boogie board and rode the waves.

At lunchtime, Max decided to have a picnic on top of a jetty. He climbed the rocks, then found what he thought would be a good spot.

Max spread out his chips, his sandwich, and his juice.

All of a sudden a large gull swooped down and grabbed half of Max's sandwich. Another gull grabbed some chips.

Max thought,

maybe if I find a different spot,
the gulls will leave me alone.

As he climbed a dune,
he heard his dad yell . . .

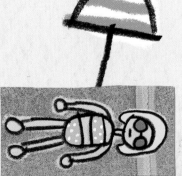

Max sat.

But not for long!